THE CROCODILE WHO LOST HIS GLASSES

AND OTHER STORIES

GILES EKINS

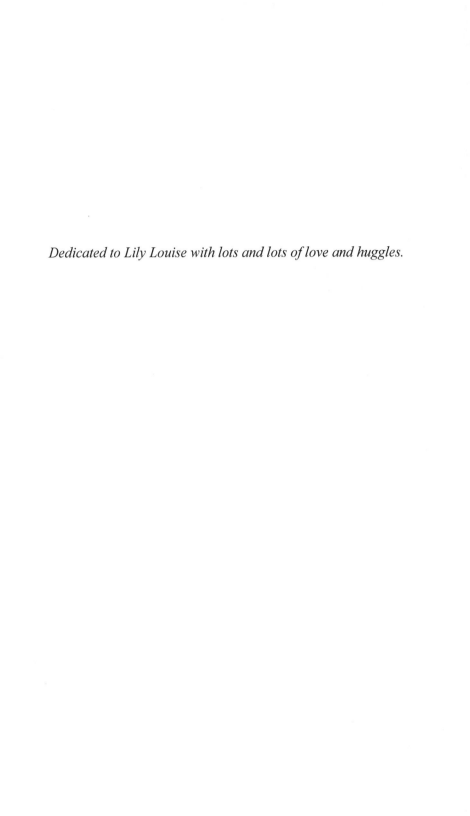

Dedicated to Lily Louise with lots and lots of love and huggles.

CONTENTS

THE CROCODILE WHO LOST HIS GLASSES

Once upon a time, there was a crocodile called Cranberry who lived in a little house on the bank of a river in Africa.

One morning, Cranberry woke up but could not find his glasses anywhere. He searched and searched everywhere, but still could not find them.

He looked under the bed, under his pillow. He looked in the bathroom, behind the sofa in the living room and he looked in all the cupboards in the kitchen.

He even looked in the smelly rubbish bin, holding his long nose as he rummaged through the potato peelings, fish heads and very stinky old cheese. But he still could not find his glasses.

'I had better go and look for them,' he thought.

Off he set along the riverbank, looking from side to side in case he had dropped his glasses somewhere. Then he met Horace the Hippo.

'Hello, Horace,' he called.

'Hello, Cranberry,' said Horace. 'What are you doing here?'

'I've lost my glasses and I'm looking for them.'

'Well, where did you lose them?'

'If I knew that, they wouldn't be lost, would they?' Cranberry answered.

'No, I suppose not,' Horace said, and he waddled down to the river to look for some fresh river grass to eat. Horace was very, very good at eating.

Silly hippo, thought Cranberry and carried on walking.

HARRY THE LAUGHING HYENA was standing by a tree, laughing and giggling to himself as usual.

'Hello, Harry,' said Cranberry.

'Oh, hello, Cranberry,' said Harry, 'what are you doing out here?'

'I've lost my glasses and I'm trying to find them.'

'Well, when you find them, you'll be able to look for them, won't you?' said Harry and he ran off, laughing crazily at his own silly joke.

Silly hyena, thought Cranberry.

NEXT, Cranberry met Alan the Anteater.

'You've lost your glasses?' Alan said. 'Where?

'I don't know.' Cranberry answered.

'OK, but when you find them, why don't you come with me and look for ants? Lovely, delicious ants, you will love them as they wriggle around in your tummy.'

'No, thank you, Alan, I don't think I'd like ants to eat.'

'Won't like ants? How can anybody not like ants?' Alan the Anteater said as he trundled away, long nose on the ground, looking for his delicious ants, muttering, 'How can anybody not like ants, how can anybody not like ants?'

Silly anteater, thought Cranberry.

. . .

'WHO'S THAT?' asked Ronald the Rhino, peering and squinting at Cranberry as rhinoceroses have very poor eyesight.

'It's me, Cranberry the Crocodile,'

'Cranberry? What are you doing here?'

'I've lost my glasses and I'm looking for them.'

'Glasses? What do you need glasses for?' Ronald asked.

'I need them to find my food. To catch fish.'

'I don't need glasses to find *my* food, so why do you?' Ronald asked, puzzled as to why anybody needed glasses to find food.

'Ronald, you eat grass,' Cranberry answered, and he lifted his head to look around. All he could see for miles around was grassland in every direction. 'Grass is everywhere,' he said, 'all around you. You don't need to look for it because it's already there.'

'Oh, I suppose so,' Ronald mumbled and he walked away, munching on another mouthful of fresh grass. 'Glasses,' he muttered, 'glasses, who needs glasses?'

Silly rhinoceros, thought Cranberry.

GEOFFREY THE GIRAFFE was no help, either. He was standing by a tall acacia tree, eating the fresh green leaves at the top.

'Hello, Geoffrey!' Cranberry shouted.

Geoffrey looked down to see Cranberry standing at the foot of the tree.

'Oh, it's you, Cranberry. What are you doing so far from the river?'

'I've lost my glasses and I'm looking for them.'

'They are not up here. Why would you think your glasses could be here at the top of a tree?'

'No, I just wondered if you had seen them, that's all.'

'No, no glasses up here.'

Silly giraffe, thought Cranberry.

ELSA THE ELEPHANT was standing in a dust bowl, picking up dust with her trunk and throwing it over her back as a sunscreen.

'Oh, hello, Cranberry,' she said. 'What are you doing here?'

'I've lost my glasses and I'm looking for them.'

'Lost your glasses?' Elsa said, throwing some more dust over her back. The dust got into Cranberry's nose and he sneezed, and his false teeth shot out from his mouth.

'Oh, I'm sorry,' said Elsa. She picked up his false teeth with her trunk and, after wiping them clean on some grass, handed them back to Cranberry. 'What sharp teeth you have.'

'Thank you, but that doesn't help find my glasses, does it?'

Elsa looked around. 'No, sorry, I can't see them,' she said. 'Anyway, I'm going down to the pool to wallow in some mud. Do you want to come with me?'

'No, I'm not going to find my glasses in a mud pool, am I?'

'No, I suppose not,' Elsa said and trundled off down to the mud pool.

Silly elephant, Cranberry said, but he was really very fond of Elsa the Elephant.

CRANBERRY WALKED ON FURTHER, passing under another tall tree.

'Hello Cranberry,' he heard somebody call to him. He looked up and saw Lily the Leopard, lying stretched out along a branch of the tree, her long tail slowly swinging to and fro.

'Oh, hello, Lily,' Cranberry said peering up at her.

'What are you doing so far from the river?' Lily asked.

'I've lost my glasses and I've been looking all over for them.'

'Your glasses? They're there!'

'Where?' exclaimed Cranberry, looking around.

'There. On top of your head.'

Cranberry felt around the top of his head with his claws and sure enough, there were his glasses! He pulled them down onto his nose and at last he could see clearly.

'Oh, thank you, Lily,' he said, 'thank you.'

Silly crocodile, thought Lily fondly as she watched Cranberry happily walking back towards his little house by the river.

LILY AND MR TURTLE

Lily, who was five, lived with her mummy and daddy and her grandad, who had no teeth and talked to himself a lot.

They lived in a lovely little house on the edge of the Dark Woods and from her bedroom window, Lily could see the foxes and badgers, the squirrels and the birds who lived there and she would wave to them every morning and every night.

Her house was quite a long way away from the nearest village where Lily went to school, but she didn't mind the walk.

As she walked to school, she would often stop and talk to the horses and cows and sheep in the fields as she passed.

She would talk to the magpies and crows and rooks and sometimes to Ollie the Owl, who lived in a hole in a big oak tree nearby.

But one bright, sunny morning, she spent too long talking to Ollie the Owl and realised that she was going to be late for school.

Lily started to run but, in her hurry, she tripped over a big stone and twisted her leg as she fell.

'Oh dear, that does look painful,' Ollie said, as Lily began to hobble slowly away.

'It is very painful,' Lily replied, 'and I can't walk very fast at all. I am going to be *so* late for school. What am I going to do?'

'I'm sorry,' Ollie said, 'but I'm afraid I can't help you,' and he flew away back to his home in the oak tree.

'I'm going to be so, *so* late for school,' Lily said again, as she hobbled down the road.

Just then, she met Mr Turtle. He was a very big, very old turtle. He was nearly as big as Lily's daddy when he got down on his hands and knees to give her a ride on his back.

'Hello, little girl,' Mr Turtle said. 'Have you hurt your leg?'

'Yes and I'm on my way to school and I'm going to be *so* late!'

'Would you like me to give you a lift?'

'Oh, yes please, would you?'

'Of course,' said Mr Turtle and so Lily climbed up on the turtle's back and off they set.

But very slowly.

Very, *very* slowly.

Plod, plod, plod, went Mr Turtle, stopping now and then to eat some grass, or a few bright yellow dandelions.

'Oh, please,' Lily said, 'can't you go a little faster?'

'Faster? *Faster*? Why do you want to go faster?'

'Because I'm going to be late.'

'I don't know. All you young people, dashing here, dashing there, never stopping to enjoy the view or taste the grass,' Mr Turtle said, before crossing over to the other side of the road where he had seen some more fresh, green grass.

'But I'm going to school and haven't got time to enjoy the view and I don't eat grass.'

'Don't eat grass? Whatever is the world coming to?' said Mr Turtle, but he finished his mouthful of grass and set off again.

Pod, plod, plod, plod, very, very slowly.

'Please hurry,' Lily said.

'In a hurry, in a rush, don't know why there's such a fuss!' Mr Turtle replied, as he stopped once more to eat some daisies.

'I'm going to be so late and I'll get into trouble.'

'Trouble, trouble, boil my bubble,' Mr Turtle said, as he slowly set off again.

'Please, can't you just go just a little bit faster?' Lily asked politely.

'Steady and slow. Steady and slow. You'll get there in the end, you know,' the turtle answered as he plodded along.

By now, Lily was very worried. She hated being late. She hated missing school.

'Please, please don't stop again,' she said, as Mr Turtle crossed over the road again to look at some tasty weeds.

'Oh, very well,' he said with a reluctant sigh, and carried on.

'Slow and steady, that's the way, slow and steady and we'll get there when we're good and ready,' he said, as trudged along with Lily still riding on his back.

At last, after what had seemed ages and ages and ages, they arrived at the school gates.

'Oh, thank you so much, Mr Turtle,' Lily said as she climbed down.

'You're most welcome, little girl. I quite enjoyed your company, even though you are always in a rush,' he said, wandering off toward another clump of grass.

Lily hurried into the school as fast as she could.

Miss Honeysmiles, her teacher, looked very surprised when Lily walked into the classroom. 'Oh, Lily, you are very, very, late, you know,' she said.

'I know, I'm very sorry, Miss Honeysmiles, but I hurt my leg when I was coming to school and had to take a ride with Mr Turtle who walked ever so slowly.'

'Well, Lily, it's very nearly time to go home.'

'Oh,' said Lily, 'I'm sorry.'

'Never mind, Lily. As you have made such a great effort to

get here with you poorly leg, I am going to give you a very special gold sticker, just for you.'

'Oh, thank you, Miss Honeysmiles, thank you,' Lily said, very pleased.

And then it was time to go home.

Once outside the school, she saw Mr Turtle again, who said, 'Hello, little girl, would you like a lift home?'

Lily was about to say, 'Yes, please,' even though she knew it would take ever such a long time and her mummy and daddy would be very worried, when Mr Wolf, a friend of the family, said, 'Hello, Lily, I can give you a lift home if you like?'

'Oh, yes please, Mr Wolf, would you?'

And so Lily climbed onto Mr Wolf's back and in no time at all they had reached Lily's house at the edge of the Dark Woods.

'Thank you so much, Mr Wolf, ' Lily said.

'My pleasure, Lily,' and off he ran into the trees.

Lily told her Mummy and Daddy and Grandad all about her adventures and Mummy washed and bandaged her leg and in the morning it was so much better.

So she was able to walk school, but made sure that she did not spend too long talking to the cows and horses and sheep, and especially to Ollie the Owl.

THE LEOPARD WHO LOST HER SPOTS

L ily the Leopard lived in a little house on the plains of Africa.

She was a very popular leopard and had lots and lots and lots of friends.

There was Cranberry the Crocodile, Geoffrey the Giraffe, Harry the Hyena, Ronald the Rhino and her very best friend, Elsa the Elephant.

Lily was very proud of her lovely spotted fur and would often go to the pond to admire them in the reflection.

'What lovely spots,' she would say, and all her friends agreed that Lily had the loveliest, spottiest fur that they had ever seen.

Until one morning, she woke up to find that all her lovely spots had gone. Disappeared!

What on earth had happened to her spots?

She looked all around her bed.

She looked under her bed.

She looked in the kitchen and behind the sofa.

She looked up the tree where she sat to watch the world go by.

But no leopard spots could be seen anywhere.

Lily asked all her friends, 'Have you seen my spots?' and they all shook their heads. 'No, sorry, Lily we haven't seen any spots at all.'

'Will you help me find them, please?' she asked.

All her friends said, 'Yes, of course, Lily.'

And so Cranberry the Crocodile, Geoffrey the Giraffe, Harry the Hyena, Ronald the Rhino and Elsa the Elephant looked everywhere that they could think of.

Cranberry looked in the river.

Geoffrey looked up at the tops of the trees.

Harry Hyena ran round in circles, giggling and laughing to himself, but found nothing.

Ronald the Rhino searched in the tall grass whilst Elsa the Elephant looked down by the mud hole.

But no leopard spots at all were found.

Not even one tiny little spot.

Lily was so upset. She did not know what to do about her lovely missing spots.

'Why not go and see the Leopard Queen?' suggested Elsa. 'She must know everything about leopard spots!'

'What a good idea,' Lily said. 'The Leopard Queen must be able to help me.'

And so she walked all across the plains until she reached Leopard Mountain, where the Leopard Queen lived.

'What do you want?' growled a leopard guard outside the cave where the Queen met visitors.

'I've come to see Leonora, the Leopard Queen, to see if she can help me,' replied Lily.

'Why should the Leopard Queen help you? You're not a leopard!'

'I am! I am a leopard, only I lost my spots and I hope the Queen can help me find them.'

'Wait here. I'll see if Her Majesty will see you, but I doubt it. Whoever heard of a leopard losing their spots?'

Lily waited anxiously until the guard returned.

'Come,' he growled and led Lily into the cave.

Leonora the Leopard Queen sat on her throne, a crown upon her head.

She stared at Lily for a long time before saying in a deep, angry voice, 'A leopard who loses his or her spots, is not a leopard. You are no longer to be called a leopard and you are forbidden by leopard law to call yourself a leopard. You are hereby banished from the noble family of leopards. Now, go and never return unless you have the spots necessary to be considered a leopard.'

Lily was so upset that she cried all the way home.

'Whatever am I going to do?' she asked her friends. 'How can I ever be a leopard again? I'm nobody. Nothing.'

All the friends got together to give Lily a hug.

Then Elsa said, 'I have an idea. Wait here,' and off she trundled to Mr Jones' ostrich farm.

A little while later, Elsa came back carrying a pot of paint and a paint brush in her trunk.

'Mr Jones was painting his daughter's bicycle and I asked if I could have some paint. Lily, we are going to paint some spots on you so that you can become a leopard again.

And that was what she did, covering Lily's fur in lovely new spots.

'Oh, thank you, Elsa!' Lily cried and set off across the plains again to see the Leopard Queen.

The Leopard Queen took a long, hard look at Lily's new spots and went to talk to some other older leopards.

Lily felt very nervous until the Leopard Queen came back.

'Leopard law does not state what colour a leopard's spot are supposed to be,' said the Queen, 'and so there is nothing to prevent you from being called a leopard again. Even if your spots are pink!'

Lily was so happy that she ran all the way back home to tell her friends the good news.

THE PHANTOM CROCODILE OF THE OPERA

'I want a tiger cub. You promised me a tiger cub, Daddy!' the boy shouted at his father, the famous explorer. 'Where is it?' he demanded.

The boy, who was called Pierre, was a horrid little boy. He was spoilt, bad-tempered, demanding and greedy. If he was given a sweet, he wanted two. If given two, he wanted four. If given four, he wanted the whole packet and when he was given a bicycle for his birthday, he shouted that he wanted *two* bicycles. Nothing he was given was ever enough.

'Where's my tiger cub?' he shouted again.

'I did try to find you a tiger cub,' the father said, 'really I did, but there simply aren't any tigers in Africa. Not one.'

'I don't care, Daddy. I WANT A TIGER CUB AND I WANT IT NOW!' he shouted, stamping his feet.

'I did bring you a crocodile instead, Pierre, a lovely baby crocodile.'

'I don't want a stupid baby crocodile; I wanted a tiger cub. You promised!'

'I know, but just have a look at the crocodile. She's lovely, she's called Chloe and I'm sure you will love her every bit as much as a tiger cub.'

'I won't. I hate it. And hate you, Daddy, you're hateful, mean and never ever give anything me that I want. Ever.'

Pierre snatched the baby crocodile from his father's hand, ran out of the house into the street and thrust it roughly through the bars of the grating and into the drains. The bars had a very sharp edge which cut deeply across Chloe's nose and face, but Pierre did not care. He really was a very horrid child.

'There, it's gone!' he shouted. 'Now go and get me a tiger cub.'

CHLOE LANDED in the waters of the drain. It had been raining heavily and she was swept away by the rushing water.

The drain soon led into another larger drain and then into a still larger drain, which then flowed into a river. The river carried Chloe along until it flowed into a cavern with a large lake in the middle. At the edge of the lake, Chloe could see some steps leading up to a walkway, so she swam across and climbed out, deciding that she would like to stay by the lake. She felt safe, there were plenty of fish to eat and, most importantly, there were no horrid little boys.

After a while, Chloe decided to explore her new home. At the end of the walkway, she found a narrow tunnel and more steps leading upwards. She climbed up the steps, coming to lots of cellars and stores with even more stairs leading upwards. The cavern with the lake was obviously underneath a very large building.

She climbed up the next set of stairs and peered round the corner. There were lots of men and women in costumes and she could hear music and singing. *Lovely* music and singing! She stayed listening for a long time, entranced by the beautiful sounds. *I wish I could sing like that*, she thought, as she made her way back down to her lake.

One day, when Chloe was in the lake looking for fish, her head became entangled with a white plastic bag that a careless, stupid human had thrown into the river. No matter how hard she struggled, pulling and tugging at the bag with her claws, she could not get it off her head. But she did bite holes big enough to breathe and scratched out holes so that she could see.

Oh well, it's like a mask, she thought, *and at least it will hide the scar on my face.*

As time passed, Chloe grew and grew until she became a fully grown adult crocodile, but she always made sure she was never seen, keeping to the shadows and dark corners. And whenever she could, she listened to all the lovely music and all the beautiful singing. And one day, she realised that she must be underneath the famous Opera House in Paris.

And as Chloe listened to the words and music, she found that without realising it, she had memorised all those lovely words and the beautiful tunes. And so, down by the lake, she started to sing to herself, listening as her voice echoed around the walls of the cavern, without appreciating just how beautiful her voice was.

She did not think she could be heard, but her pure voice carried all the way up those stairs and onto the stage of the opera house.

'Who is that singing?' everybody asked.

'Such beautiful singing. Who can it be?'

'It must be the Phantom of the Opera,' exclaimed one actor.

'There is no such thing as the Phantom of the Opera,' said another.

'But who is that singing? If it is not one of us, it must be the Phantom.'

'Yes, it must be the Phantom.'

'If it is the Phantom, we must find him,' Mr Buffoon, the opera house manager, said.

So everybody, the singers, actors and the back-stage staff, was ordered to search for the phantom.

They looked in every room, behind the stage, above the stage, in the changing rooms, in the cellars and although they could still hear the singing, they had no idea where it was coming from.

Eventually, a few brave actors made their way down to the lake, shining their torches all around, but Chloe had heard them coming and slid into the water, hiding in the farthest, darkest corner.

As soon as they had gone back upstairs, Chloe came out of the lake and started singing again.

'It can only be the Phantom, we've looked everywhere possible,' the fat leading soprano, Madame Pomposity, told Mr Buffoon.

'There is no phantom, it must be somebody who hides when we come near,' Mr Boney Skellington, the very tall, skinny leading tenor, said.

'It must be an angel,' somebody else said.

'Such lovely singing, such a lovely voice,' said Mr Buffoon. 'If only I could find out who is singing, I would cast them as the leading lady in all the operas.'

Madame Pomposity did not look happy at that. 'Whoever it is, she does not have the voice. She sounds like a squealing pig.'

'You should know. Have you heard yourself sing?' retorted Mr Boney Skellington.

Madame Pomposity and Mr Boney Skellington did not get on, as each of them thought that they were the most important singer.

It was Percy the stage cat who found Chloe. She was singing an aria from a famous opera called *Madame Butterfly*, and did not hear Percy as he approached because, being a cat, he walks very quietly.

'Hello,' he said when Chloe finished the song. 'Everybody has been looking for you. You sing so, so beautifully,'

'But I'm a crocodile! How can a crocodile sing beautifully? Crocodiles just grunt and croak.'

'No, really, truly, you have the most beautiful voice that has ever been heard in the famous Paris Opera House. Everybody says so.'

'No, they don't, I've heard them. They think I'm a phantom.'

'Listen to me. What's your name by the way?'

'Chloe. Chloe the croaking crocodile.'

'No, listen Chloe, you do not croak, you sing so wonderfully that the manager wants you to sing in all the operas.'

'But I'm ugly – so ugly that I have to wear a mask to hide my scarred face. Who would want to watch that?'

'People come to hear the singing and your voice is so pure and perfect, they will not notice your scars or your mask.'

'Do you think so?'

'I know so. Please come with me and meet Mr Buffoon, the manager and sing for him.'

'OK, but I know he'll only laugh, because whoever heard of a singing crocodile?'

Nevertheless, Percy led Chloe into Mr Buffoon's office. 'Here is your phantom, she has come to sing for you,' he announced proudly.

'Oh, it's a phantom crocodile,' Mr Buffoon joked. 'Do please sing,' he said sarcastically. Obviously, he did not believe that a crocodile was able sing opera.

But when Chloe sang some of the songs she had learned, Mr Buffoon was so impressed that he immediately cast her in one of the operas, deciding to promote her appearance with posters and advertisements which read:

MADAME BUTTERFLY
Starring
CHLOE
THE PHANTOM CROCODILE OF THE OPERA

She was a sensation, an overnight success.

One night, Pierre, the horrid little boy who had now grown up to be a horrid little man, was sitting in the audience with his father. As soon as Chloe began to sing, he stood up and shouted, 'Father, I want that singing crocodile. Get it for me. GET IT FOR ME NOW!'

But horrid little boys who grow into horrid little men don't always get want they want, do they?

THE ELEPHANT WHO FORGOT

E lephants never forget, you know. They always know where to find the waterholes with the sweetest water, where to find the trees with the juiciest leaves, which were the muddiest mud holes in which to roll and relax and how to find their way across the vast plains of Africa.

Elephants are amongst the cleverest of animals, but Erasmus was by far the cleverest elephant in the world. He was so clever; he might even be the cleverest creature in the world. Cleverer even than the cleverest human. Cleverer even than the smartest computer.

He could tell the time by looking at buffalo poo and he could tell when it was Christmas Day by looking at the stars, even when the sky was completely cloudy. He knew the name and history of every single elephant who had ever been born, going all the way back to Tembe the Great, the very first elephant ever, thousands of years ago.

He had read every book in every language that had ever been written, memorising every single word.

He could speak every language in the world as well as seventy-four languages that he had invented.

Erasmus knew the name of every tree, every flower, every insect and every reptile in the world.

He could count backwards from 1,000 million faster than the fastest computer. He could carry out complicated mathematical problems that even the most advanced computers in the world could not solve.

Erasmus could recall every word that anybody had ever spoken to him and he could even remember what you had said before you even said it.

He could recite every play written by William Shakespeare and could act out in every role, including the scenery.

There are a hundred thousand million stars in the Milky Way and Erasmus knew that name of every single one.

And he never forgot anything. Nothing. He remembered everything he had ever learned from the day he was born.

EVERYTHING!

However, because he was so very, very clever, his brain was HUGE. So huge that his head was two times larger and two times heavier than the head of any other elephant…

Which was a GREAT BIG PROBLEM!

Because you see, his head was so big and heavy, Erasmus had to grow tusks that reached down to the ground in order to support his very heavy, brainy head. These tusks were so long that when he walked, they would scrape along the ground, making tracks wherever he went, digging up worms and beetles for the birds to eat.

Which was all very well for the birds, but very uncomfortable and tiring for Erasmus.

It was his clever granddaughter, Emily Elephant, who thought of a solution to this problem. She fastened a discarded skateboard to each of Erasmus' tusks, right at the point where the tusks touched the ground.

Which, for Erasmus, made walking very much easier and

much less tiring. But the birds were not so happy, as the ready supply of worms dried up.

And then something most extraordinary started to happen.

Erasmus, the cleverest elephant in the world, had begun to forget things. This caused a huge sensation amongst the elephants, because, as I told you, an elephant NEVER forgets. Especially Erasmus.

It was simple things that he forgot. He could not remember how a nursery rhyme went. He could sing, 'Hickory dickory dock. The mouse ran up the...' but that was as far as he could remember.

He had forgotten which planet was closest to the sun – which, as you know, is Mercury.

Erasmus could not remember which was his favourite mud hole and went to one that had dried up twenty years ago.

He forgot to brush his teeth at night and to pick out the fluff between his toe nails, as well as forgetting to wipe his bottom after he had been to the toilet and washing his trunk before he ate.

It was only when he forgot his own name that the Elephant Queen called together the Grand Council of Elephants to discuss this very serious matter. Because, if Erasmus could forget things, then possibly all the other elephants might forget important things, too.

Something had to be done. The discussions by the council lasted all day and all night. And achieved absolutely nothing. None of the elephants could agree what the problem was and how it could be treated.

It was Erasmus's granddaughter, Emily Elephant, who decided to investigate, to find out what the problem was with her grandfather.

She looked into his eyes, looked inside his mouth and examined his poo. She did not know why she did that, but it was something to do. She peered up his trunk and looked inside his ears, scraping out the ear wax with a plastic spoon she had found, thrown away by a careless human. And it was then that she saw it.

'Grandad,' she exclaimed, 'You've got a hole in your head. That's why all your knowledge and memories are disappearing. They're leaking out through this hole!'

'A hole in my head? How very unusual! I can't recall anything like that in all of elephant history,' Erasmus said, shaking his head, which sent a few more memories flying away.

'You must stop doing that, Grand ad. Don't shake your head again, it only loosens memories so that they leak out,'

'Must stop doing what?' Erasmus asked, already forgetting what it was he was not supposed to do.

'We had better mend that hole, hadn't we? Now, you stay here and don't move. And don't shake your head, understand?'

'Yes, yes, of course I understand,' Erasmus said, shaking his head up and down in agreement.

Emily Elephant made her way into the jungle, looking for some of those trees that ooze out a sticky resin, a sort of sticky gum, and when she found them, she collected the resin in a plastic bucket that a child had thrown away. When she had filled the cup with resin, she went back to find her grandfather, only to find he had wandered off somewhere.

'Where has that silly elephant gone?' she wondered and went to look for him. She found him down by the water hole with a bunch of teenage elephants who were dancing to music coming from a radio that a tourist must have left behind. Erasmus was there in the middle of the group, jumping up and down, shaking his head wildly to the beat as his trunk waved and pounded to the rhythm.

'Oh, silly Grandad,' Emily said fondly. 'Come with me, we've got to fix that hole in your head before everything leaks out of your brain.

Emily had also found a piece of discarded purple plastic

sheeting and, with the help of Cranberry the Crocodile, she had managed to cut it to size, about twelve inches square. She smeared the sticky resin onto the plastic patch and onto Erasmus head where the hole was. She then stuck the patch over the hole and held it in place until it had dried, very effectively sealing the hole.

'Oh, that is wonderful, amazing!' said Erasmus. 'I can remember things. I can remember all those things that I thought I'd forgotten. They hadn't all escaped. Spare copies of those memories and knowledge had been stored in the back of my mind but the leaks had disturbed everything in my brain, making it difficult to remember,'

And so, with Emily Elephant's help, Erasmus was once again the cleverest elephant in the world, quite possibly the cleverest elephant ever, the cleverest *creature* ever!

And he did not mind one bit that he had a bright purple patch on the side of his head.

THE SKUNK WHO LOST HIS STINK

E very year, all the skunks in the country would gather together to hold a competition to find out who was the smelliest skunk of all and be crowned as the World's Champion Stinker. And every year Skorpio won. He really was the smelliest, stinkiest skunk that anyone had ever known. Or smelled.

He was so stinky that grass withered and leaves crumpled up and died as he passed by.

He was so smelly that onions he touched no longer smelled or tasted of onion, but of skunk.

He was stinkier than the stinkiest farts you have ever smelled. Even smellier than yours. Or Grandad's.

He was so stinky that even other skunks had to hold their noses when he was nearby.

He was so smelly that birds fell out of the trees in a faint when he walked past.

Skorpio was ready for the big competition. He was the smelliest he had ever been, so disgustingly stinky that he couldn't even stand the smell of himself.

The competition was to take place the following day and even though the smelliest, stinkiest skunks from all over the country had travelled far and wide to enter the competition, Scorpio was confident that he would win once again.

But when morning came, Skorpio could not smell anything. He sniffed but... no smell. He sniffed again loudly, but still he could not smell anything, not even the tiniest little whiff of stink.

Did he have a cold which meant he couldn't smell? Did he possibly have a blocked nose? He blew his nose on a big red and white checked handkerchief, then on some tissues, but still no smell.

He sniffed under his armpits, he sniffed behind his tail, he even held his paws against his mouth to smell his breath, which was normally disgusting, but there was no smell there, either.

What had happened? What had gone wrong? How could he win the competition if he had no stink? He had to do something and as quickly as possible, for the competition would be starting soon.

Skorpio quickly hurried away, looking for smelly things to roll in and make himself smelly.

He rolled in some cow dung.

He smeared himself with doggie-poo.

And then he dived into a pile of horse manure.

Now he was really smelly again but, as he was walking back to the competition, it began to rain. Only a few small drops to begin with, so he wasn't worried. But then the rain begin to come a bit heavier and then heavier still. Then it became a downpour and all the stinky stuff that he had rolled, smeared and dived in was completely washed away.

There was no way he could enter the competition now; everybody would just laugh at him.

Skorpio was so ashamed that he ran away and hid, watching the competition from behind a tree. To his very great annoyance, his biggest rival Skarflo won, even though he was hardly stinky at all. Skorpio watched angrily as the Stinkiest Skunk crown was placed on Skarfio's head and he was proclaimed the World's Champion Stinker.

What to do? How could Skorpio ever become smelly again? How could he get back his title as the smelliest, stinkiest skunk?

He went to consult with Smellsa, the skunk-witch.

'Please help me, Smellsa,' Skorpio begged. 'I've lost all my smell and I can never ever win the title of smelliest skunk unless I can get all my stinkiness back.'

Smellsa examined Skorpio from head to tail, sniffing and smelling at him all the time. 'Hmmm,' she said after her examination, 'you are suffering from no-smellie-itus.'

'No-smellie-itus, what's that'

'It's caused by a poor diet, constipation, flatulence, worms, good breath and too much washing. Oh, and somebody's put a bad spell on you.'

'That must be Skarfio, it's the only way he could win. But what can I do? Is there a cure?'

'I can remove the bad spell, easy-peasy, sugar is greasy, but you'll have to go into the jungle to cure the no-smellie-itus yourself.'

'How do I do that?'

'Deep in the jungle, you will find a flower called titan alum. It is the smelliest flower in the world. It is also the tallest, so you had better take a ladder with you. But be careful, this flower only blooms once every seven years and then only for forty-eight hours. Miss it and you won't smell again for seven years.'

Smellsa then sprinkled some yellow dust over Skorpio. 'Right,' she said, 'that has removed the bad spell. It has bounced back onto Skarfio and he will be without his stink for almost a year. But if you want to win next year, you must find that titan alum and rub yourself with the flower. Then your own stink will start to work again.'

'Thank you, Smellsa,' Skorpio said and paid for his treatment with a bunch of rotten bananas, a handful of dead flies and a piece of old chewing gum he had found trodden onto the pavement.

Then he set out for the jungle.

For seven days and seven nights he searched for that elusive flower, but without success. He was about to give up, thinking that Smellsa had played a trick on him. Skunk-witches do that all the time, don't they?

But then at last he found it. It was a tall, green plant that looked like a spear. But was he too late? Had it flowered already and would not flower again for seven years?

What to do? He dare not go away in case he missed it flowering, so he sat at the side of the flower, waiting and watching. And he watched and waited. And waited and watched some more. Then he was so tired of waiting, he fell asleep and almost missed it when the flower did bloom.

It was the vilest stink he had ever smelled that woke him up. It was even smellier than he had been when at his smelliest. He set up his ladder and climbed up to the top of the flower and rubbed himself all over with the smelly petals.

How wonderful to feel stinky again!

Skorpio stayed by the flower for all the forty-eight hours that it bloomed, continuously rubbing himself with the petals until the flower suddenly closed up, almost trapping his nose as it did so. That was it for another seven years.

With all that stink from the titan alum on his fur, he also began to feel that his own stink was working again and so, by the time the competition came round again, he was once again the smelliest, stinkiest skunk of all.

He easily won the competition. He was named as the World's Champion Stinker and, best of all, Skarfio came last.

Skorpio, the smelliest, stinkiest skunk, was also now the happiest skunk and when he went to bed that night, he slept still wearing his crown.

THE ELEPHANT WHO LOST HER TRUNK

Elsa the Elephant lived on the plains of Africa in a pretty little thatched house down by the river. Her cousin Emily Elephant lived nearby and she had lots and lots of friends including Cranberry the Crocodile, Horace the Hippo, Harry the Laughing Hyena, Ronald the Rhino, Geoffrey the Giraffe and Lily the Leopard.

She was the happiest elephant there had ever been. She loved disco dancing, needlework and making pretty pictures out of elephant poo. In fact, one of her poo pictures had been found by a tourist who had been so impressed that he had collected it and, without her knowledge, submitted it to an art gallery in London where it won lots of prizes.

Elsa just thought that the poo-picture had been washed away in the rains.

One morning, just after her birthday, Elsa went down to the river to get a drink. It was a hot day and she was very, very, thirsty.

She dipped the end of her trunk into the river, sucked up some water and squirted it into her mouth. And then again.

But she was so busy drinking, she did not notice a crocodile slyly swimming closer and closer and closer towards her.

He crept closer still, with just his eyes and nostrils showing above the water.

And the next time she dipped her trunk into the river, Snowball the Crocodile, who was Cranberry's brother, leapt up out of the water and bit Elsa's trunk clean off and raced away up the river with it.

'Gwanberr!' she shouted, 'Schnowbaa hath spitten by trunk orr!' (Meaning 'Cranberry, Snowball has bitten my trunk off!')

'What?' Cranberry shouted, racing towards her as fast as he could. 'Snowball, my brother, has bitten your trunk off? Is that what you said?'

'Yeth, canth ooo eee?' (Can't you see?)

'Yes, sorry,' Cranberry said, straightening his glasses that had come loose as he ran to Elsa. 'I have to say that Snowball has always been a bad crocodile, even though he is my brother. Don't worry, we'll get your trunk back.'

'Dank oo,' Elsa said, tears in her eyes that she could not wipe away without her trunk.

Elsa's cousin Emily came over and wrapped her trunk around Elsa to comfort her, whilst Cranberry shouted to Lily the Leopard, who had now joined the throng of friends coming to Elsa's aid.

'Lily, you are the fastest one of us, you run along the river bank and follow Snowball wherever he goes. Harry,' he said to the hyena, 'you follow Snowball on the other side of the river in case he tries to get away on that side.'

Lily and Harry raced away as fast as they could to follow Snowball, as he fled up the river with Elsa's trunk still in his jaws.

Cranberry then shouted to the hippo. 'Horace, you come with me. We'll swim upriver after Snowball.'

'What about me?' asked Ronald the Rhino, peering short-sightedly towards Cranberry.

'You stay here with Elsa and comfort her. Your eyesight is not really good enough to help track Snowball down.'

'OK,' Ronald said. He was disappointed not to help in the chase, but he understood why he could not, as he could barely see Elsa standing ten yards away! All rhinos have very poor eyesight but have an excellent sense of smell.

'Geoffrey,' Cranberry said to the giraffe, 'can you run up to the top of that hill over there? See if you can see Snowball, and see where he is going to. If you spot him, give us a shout, or wave your head in the right direction.'

'Yes, yes, of course.'

Having given his instructions, Cranberry dived into the river and began his pursuit of his brother, followed by Horace the Hippo. However, Horace, although a good swimmer, was not as fast as Cranberry and so he soon fell behind but he carried on, determined to do the best he could to help his friend Elsa.

Meanwhile, Snowball, noticing that Lily the Leopard was following on one side of the river and that Harry the Hyena was following on the other side and, certain that Cranberry would be swimming after him as fast as he could, he decided that he would hide for a while. He found a narrow stream with lots of reeds and overhanging trees and hid himself away where he could not be seen.

With only his eyes showing, he waited in hiding until he saw Cranberry frantically swimming upstream. Thinking it now safe, he slowly slid out from his hiding place and began to swim downstream, in the opposite direction from where Lily, Harry, Geoffrey and Cranberry were searching.

However, he had not gone very far when he came across Horace, still swimming upstream in pursuit.

'Snowball!' Horace shouted angrily. 'How dare you attack my friend Elsa! Give me back her trunk. Give it back *now*!'

Snowball said nothing. He tried to get past Horace, but the angry hippo blocked him whichever way he tried to get past.

'Give me Elsa's trunk!' he shouted again, blocking Snowball once again with his large body. All the shouting and splashing as Snowball tried to get past alerted three or four of the other hippos in the river and they quickly swam along to help Horace. Snowball, now realizing he was trapped, dropped Elsa's trunk and scrambled up the bank and ran away, never to be seen again.

Horace carefully picked up Elsa's trunk and hurriedly swam back to Elsa, who was still being comforted by Emily Elephant and Ronald the Rhino.

'Here we are, Elsa,' he said. 'I've managed to get it away from Snowball.'

'Dank oo, uttt ow go schpit it ack on?' (Thank you but how am I going to stick it back on?)

'Oh,' said Horace, 'I never thought about that.'

Emily shouted to Geoffrey up on the hill. 'Geoffrey, tell Cranberry, Harry and Lily to come back, Horace has rescued Elsa's trunk.

When all the friends were back, they tried various ways to stick Elsa's trunk back on.

First of all, they tried spit but that did not work.

Next, they tried some mud and although that worked for a while, as soon as the mud dried, it cracked and the trunk fell off.

'Ot ee oona oo?' wailed Elsa. (What are we going to do?)

All the friends sat around trying to think of ways to help, but some of the ideas were either too silly. Cranberry wanted to nail the trunk back on. Geoffrey suggested hanging heavy weights on what was left of Elsa's trunk and stretching it, but Elsa shook her head violently. No, no, no.

Emily Elephant found some sticky gum from a tree, but it stung too much and Elsa did not like the taste, so that didn't work.

It was Lily the Leopard who finally solved the problem. She

happened to glance across towards the trees and saw some bright yellow birds called weaver birds.

'That's it!' she said and ran over to talk to them. Weaver birds build elaborate nests, stitching grass and sinewy strands into nests that hang like balls from the branches of trees, with a small entrance at the bottom. Some nests even have a long tube woven to the bottom to further protect the entrance and safeguard their chicks.

Lily spoke to Wellstitch, the weaver bird who had built the best nest and explained the situation, that Elsa's trunk needed to be sewn back on. 'Would the weaver birds help?' she asked.

'Of course we will,' Wellstitch answered and he called all the weaver birds together and sent them out to find strong reeds, or locate sinewy plants, or find pieces of strings or other useful things that humans might have left behind.

All the friends searched for suitable material and before long, Wellstitch had everything the weaver birds needed. Together with five other very skilful weavers, Wellstitch expertly sewed Elsa's trunk back. It was so cleverly done that you could hardly see the stitches.

'Oh, thank you, thank you,' Elsa told the weaver birds and all her friends and then hurried down to the river to get a drink. She had found it difficult to get a drink without a trunk and had had to rely on Emily Elephant to squirt water into her mouth.

'Be careful,' Cranberry joked. 'Make sure that Snowball isn't around to bite it off again.'

But neither Snowball or any other mean crocodiles were there and Elsa dipped her trunk into the waters and took the longest drink ever, her mended trunk working just as well as it had before.

THE HYENA WHO LOST HER LAUGH

Hyacinth the Laughing Hyena lived on the plains of Africa with her mummy and daddy and her brothers, Hybrid, Half-inch (who was very small) and Horrid. When he was younger, Horrid had done something really disgusting and his mother said, 'That's horrid,' and the name had stuck. He was Horrid – horrid by nature and horrid by name.

After breakfast and their morning lessons, Hyacinth and her brothers would go out to play, running around, chasing each other, laughing and giggling, laughing, laughing, laughing all the time, which is why hyenas are called laughing hyenas.

But then, one morning when she woke up, Hyacinth had lost her laugh.

No matter how hard she tried, she could not laugh.

Where had her laugh gone?

She wondered whether Horrid, who was always unpleasant towards her, had taken it whilst she was asleep.

'No, no, Hyacinth, I swear I have not taken your laugh.'

Hyacinth did not know whether or not to believe him, but then he offered to help her look for her laugh. Together with her other brothers, she looked all around the little house they lived in by the river. They looked under the bed, inside the kitchen cupboards and behind the settee, but they could not find her laugh, not even the faintest little giggle.

She asked all her friends whether they had seen or heard her laugh. She asked Cranberry the Crocodile, Lily the Leopard, her cousin Harry the Hyena and Elsa the Elephant, but none of them had seen or heard her laugh and even after they had helped her to look for it, it still could not be found.

Where had it gone? How had it gone?

Hyacinth next went to see Grandad Horace, who, like all grandads, knew everything about everything. He was asleep under the shade of a tree, but Hyacinth woke him up and told him all about her lost laugh.

'You've lost your laugh?' he said very slowly and solemnly, peering at her through his very thick spectacles. 'That is a most serious matter and it will have to be taken up by the Hyena Grand Council unless you can find it. A hyena's laugh is a precious thing and not to be lost just like that.'

'But Grandad, how could I have lost it?'

'Have you been down to the Windy Canyon?' he asked.

'Yes, we all went, Hybrid, Half-inch, Horrid and me. We played down there yesterday.'

'Well, there you are. Your laugh has been blown away by the… the… the… winds. Yes, that must be it. Go back down the Windy Canyon, you'll probably find it there, maybe caught up on some thorny bushes. Yes, yes, that's the… ticket,' and then Grandad Horace went back to sleep, snoring so loudly that his spectacles fell off the end of his nose.

Hyacinth did as Grandad Horace had suggested. She looked all the way up the canyon and all the way back down again. She looked and listened at every thorny bush, at every tree and even in the large clumps of grass. But not a laugh was to be found anywhere.

She went back and told her grandfather that she had not

found her laugh in Windy Canyon and asked him where she should look next.

'You'll maybe have to go up Stormy Mountain. I've heard that laughs sometimes do get blown up there.'

'Thank you, Grandad, I'll go up there and look.'

'Take care, Hyacinth, there's a bad-tempered old mountain goat called Gotcha, up there somewhere.'

'More bad-tempered than you, Grandad?' she said with a smile, giving him a kiss on his forehead.

'Get away with you, you cheeky monkey.'

It was a long, long, climb up Stormy Mountain and she was very tired by the time she got to the top. She looked around for any sign of the bad-tempered goat but saw nothing and started to look for her missing laugh. There weren't any trees or bushes up there, but there were quite a few rocks. Perhaps her laugh had got trapped behind one of them.

As she was bending down to look behind one of the rocks, the mountain-goat ran up behind her and butted her heavily on her bottom.

'Gotcha!' shouted the goat and ran away again, laughing loudly. *Perhaps the goat has got my laugh*, she thought and ran after him, quickly catching up with him.

'Have you got my laugh?' she demanded.

'Why would I want your silly laugh? I've got my own laugh. Listen!' and Gotcha laughed loudly. It was more like a rumbling grunt that her own childish giggle. 'See, that's not your laugh, is it?'

'No, sorry, but have you seen or heard *my* laugh? I've lost it and unless I can find it again, I might not be allowed to be a Laughing Hyena.'

'Do I look as though I spend my time looking for lost hyena laughs?' Gatcha said grumpily as he walked away. 'Go and look in the Stinking Swamp.'

But her laugh was not in the Stinking Swamp and, still covered in mud, she had to go and tell Grandad Horace that she had not yet found her laugh.

'Why are you covered in mud? You're not a hippo or an elephant. Hyenas do not wallow in swamps or mud holes. Have you no pride?' asked Grandad.

'But Gotcha the mountain goat told me to look in the Stinking Swamp, Grandad.'

'Did he now? I shall have to go and have words with him, treating my granddaughter with such disrespect.'

'Never mind, Grandad, but where else shall I look?'

'That I do not know, but I shall have to report to the Hyena Grand Council now. You had better come with me to explain what has happened.'

The President of the Hyena Grand Council looked sternly down at Hyacinth. 'To lose your laugh is a serious offence. By Laughing Hyena law, you must leave our lands until such time as you find your laugh. Do not return without it.'

'But she's only a child. A *child*!' protested Grandad Horace. 'Banish me if you must, but not little Hyacinth.'

'I'm sorry, Horace, but the law is the law. This you know.'

Grandad Horace accompanied Hyacinth until they came to edge of the Hyena lands.

He gave her a hug. 'Be brave, little one. Remember you come from a proud line of distinguished Hyenas. I know you will not let us down.'

'I won't, Grandad,' and she set off across the open plains down towards the river.

There she met with some of her friends and told them what had happened.

'It's all right,' said Elsa the Elephant, 'you can come and live with us.'

Just then Elsa's little brother, Ernie, came running over, an ostrich feather held tightly in his trunk. 'Hyacinth,' Elsa said, 'this is my brother Ernie, and I've got an idea. Ernie, tickle Hyacinth's tummy with that feather.'

And he did and Hyacinth burst out laughing.

She had found her laugh at last.

GHOSTS

By
Lily Louise Ekins
(Aged 7 years)

There were 5 kids and they travelled all over the world. They went to live in a house with ghosts.

Dund. Dund. Dund.

The most smelliest ghost pushed Luke out of a window. But the most wildest thing was that Luke could now see GHOSTS!

And in the garden was a golf course, a swing, a roundabout, a rocking camel, a big dog and a big basket, a basketball court and a long, long, slide.

Luke could see all the ghosts on the slide, roundabout, rocking camel and on the swing and they were soooo, soooo happy.

You will never believe what happened next. AVA got pushed out of the window.

Then Elizabetta, Ella and I got pushed out of the window but we couldn't see the ghosts, only Luke could see ghosts and we all lived happily ever after.

THE END

Dear reader,

We hope you enjoyed reading *The Crocodile Who Lost His Glasses*. Please take a moment to leave a review, even if it's a short one. Your opinion is important to us.

Discover more books by Giles Ekins at https://www.nextchapter.pub/authors/giles-ekins

Want to know when one of our books is free or discounted? Join the newsletter at http://eepurl.com/bqqB3H

Best regards,

Giles Ekins and the Next Chapter Team

ABOUT THE AUTHOR

Giles Ekins was born in the North East of England and qualified as an Architect in London. Subsequently he spent many years living and working in Northern Nigeria, Qatar, Oman and Bahrain.

He has now returned to England and lives in Sheffield with his wife Patricia. Giles writes for both adults and children including 'The Adventures of a Travelling Cat' series, amongst other titles.

The Crocodile Who Lost His Glasses
ISBN: 978-4-86747-845-5

Published by
Next Chapter
1-60-20 Minami-Otsuka
170-0005 Toshima-Ku, Tokyo
+818035793528

27th May 2021

CPSIA information can be obtained
at www.ICGtesting.com
Printed in the USA
BVHW031525180621
609896BV00005B/154